The Emperor's New Clothes

Illustrated by Mike Gordon

Retold by Susanna Davidson
Based on a story by Hans Christian Andersen

Once upon a time there was an
Emperor who loved clothes.

He liked looking splendid
ALL the time.

He had a different outfit for every day of the year.

But the Emperor had a problem.
He had nothing to wear for
the royal procession.

"Won't any of your outfits do,
Your Highness?" asked
his servant, Boris.

"NO!" said the Emperor. "I need a
NEW outfit and I need one NOW."

"And remember – it has to be
splendid."

Boris sighed and set off to find the finest clothes-makers in town.

WANTED!
Splendid new outfit for the Emperor. Clothes-makers apply here!

NO TIME-WASTERS, PLEASE

FLOUR

He wasn't having much luck until...

a little round man

and a long thin man
rushed up to him.

They bowed with their
bottoms in the air.
"We are Slimus and
Slick, at your service,"
they said.

Boris took them to the Emperor.

"We make magic clothes," Slimus told him.
"Only clever people can see them. Stupid people can't!"

"Are they **splendid**?" asked the Emperor.
"Very **splendid**," promised Slick. "But very expensive.
We'll need pots and pots of money."

"Take all the money you want," cried the Emperor.
"Just make me those clothes!"

A week later, the Emperor and Boris went to see Slimus and Slick at work. "Welcome!" they said. "What do you think of our clothes?"

The Emperor gulped. Boris gulped.
Neither of them could see a thing.

But they didn't want to look stupid.
So the Emperor said, "Splendid!"
"Yes, really very... splendid," said Boris.

"Oh, um, er, most splendid!" added the footmen.

As soon as everyone had gone, Slimus and Slick laughed and laughed until their faces turned purple.

Then they ordered a huge feast.
"It's hungry work making magic clothes," they said.

On the morning of the
royal procession, the Emperor
couldn't wait to put on his new clothes.

"Here is your cloak," said Slimus. "It's light as a feather."

"Oh Your Highness," said Slick. "You look very handsome. Your clothes fit so well."

The Emperor admired himself in the mirror. "Don't I look *splendid?*"

"Yes, Your Highness," gasped the footmen, staring straight at the Emperor.

"Yes, Your Highness," said Boris, staring straight at the ceiling. (He was trying NOT to look.)

"Open the palace gates!" ordered the Emperor. "Let the royal procession begin."

The crowd gasped
when they saw the Emperor.
Everyone had heard that only clever
people could see his clothes.

"Aren't his clothes *splendid*?" they said.

"Let me see him!" called a small boy, who was stuck at the back of the crowd.

"Ooh!" said the boy. "The Emperor's got no clothes on!"

Faster than a spreading fire,
a whisper whizzed
through the crowd.

The Emperor heard their words. *He looked down.*
"Oh no," he thought. "I'm naked!"

Then he blushed
bright red.

"But I can't stop now. This is the royal procession and I am the Emperor."
So he held his head high and walked on.

The crowd clapped and cheered. They thought it was the most splendid royal procession ever!

Edited by Jenny Tyler and Lesley Sims
Cover design by Russell Punter

This edition first published in 2012 by Usborne Publishing Ltd, 83-85 Saffron Hill, London EC1N 8RT, England.
www.usborne.com Copyright © 2012, 2006 Usborne Publishing Ltd. The name Usborne and the devices ♈ 🎈 are Trade Marks
of Usborne Publishing Ltd.
First published in America in 2012. UE.

Look at me! Look at me!

by Rose Williamson

TOP THAT

Licensed exclusively to Top That Publishing Ltd
Tide Mill Way, Woodbridge, Suffolk, IP12 1AP, UK
www.topthatpublishing.com
Copyright © 2013 Tide Mill Media
All rights reserved
2 4 6 8 9 7 5 3 1
Manufactured in China

Illustrated by Doreen Marts
Written by Rose Williamson

ISBN 978-1-78244-218-9

A catalogue record for this book is available from the British Library

Cammy Chameleon lived in a tree and was very good at hiding. Cammy turned brown on a brown branch and green on a green leaf.

It made it very easy to
sneak up on yummy bugs!

But Cammy didn't want to hide. She thought she was a very beautiful chameleon indeed and she wanted all of the other animals to look at her.

She called out to the tree frogs, 'Look at me! Look at me!'

But the tree frogs could
not see a green chameleon
on a green leaf.

She called out to the lemurs,
'Look at me! Look at me!'

But the lemurs could not see a brown
chameleon on a brown branch.

Cammy was very upset that no one could see her.
She began to wonder what it would be like if
she didn't always blend in ...

Cammy climbed down from her tree and concentrated very, very hard ...

And turned red!

'Look at me! Look at me!'
she called to the tree frogs.
'What a beautiful chameleon!' they said.

Cammy practised changing colour all day.
She was pink on a grey stone ...

She was black on yellow sand ...

She was purple on
an orange flower ...

... and orange on
a purple flower.

'Look at me! Look at me!' she called to the lemurs. 'What a beautiful chameleon!' they said.

Cammy thought that she was the most beautiful chameleon in the whole world.

Soon, she began to feel hungry and went home to her tree.

Cammy climbed onto her brown
branch and waited for a yummy bug.
She waited and waited.

She watched the other chameleons
catching bugs on their sticky
tongues and her
stomach rumbled.
She was very hungry!

Then, Cammy saw a group of bugs nearby! But, before she could stick out her long tongue, they saw her beautiful colours and flew away!

'What a beautiful chameleon!'
the laughing bugs called to her.

Suddenly, Cammy felt very silly.
A colourful chameleon couldn't hide
like a plain brown chameleon!

Cammy knew that to catch bugs, she would need to blend in so she concentrated very, very hard ...

and changed colour so that she blended in with her surroundings!

Cammy had learnt that it is not good to show off and was happy being a regular chameleon again.

But sometimes, just every once in a while,
Cammy concentrates very, very hard ...